Scholastic's
The Magic School Bus®
Liz™
TAKES FLIGHT

by Tracey West
illustrated by Ted Enik

SCHOLASTIC INC.
New York   Toronto   London   Auckland   Sydney
Mexico City   New Delhi   Hong Kong

From the animated TV series
produced by Scholastic Productions, Inc.
Based on *The Magic School Bus* book series
written by Joanna Cole and illustrated by Bruce Degen.

By Tracey West and illustrated by Ted Enik.

ISBN 0-439-08207-2

12 11 10 9 8 7 6 5 4 3 2 1   9/9 0 1 2 3 4/0

Printed in the U.S.A.   14

First Scholastic printing, October 1999

Arnold was working very hard on his homework. "Ms. Frizzle said we have to make something fly this weekend," Arnold told Liz. "I'm going to make an airplane. You can be my pilot!"

3

Wanda came over to visit Arnold.
"I can't believe this homework assignment!" Arnold said. "I'll never get this airplane finished in time."

4

Wanda laughed. "Arnold, Ms. Frizzle never said we had to make an airplane. She just said we had to make something fly. We can use these helium balloons."

Wanda handed the balloons to Arnold.

"I can't worry about balloons right now," Arnold said. "I've got to make this plane fly!" He handed the balloons to Liz.

Why do you think helium balloons can fly?

"Arnold, no!" Wanda cried.
The balloons were flying away. And they were taking Liz with them!

7

"Hold on, Liz!" Wanda called out. Luckily, the balloons got tangled in a tree branch.

"Oh, no!" Arnold cried. "How could this happen?"

"Those balloons are filled with a gas called helium," Wanda said. "Helium is lighter than air, so that means the balloons can rise in the air."

"So why didn't *we* fly up like Liz?" Arnold asked.

"We're too heavy," Wanda explained. "Liz was just light enough for the balloons to carry her."

"What will we do now? We have to rescue Liz,"
Arnold said.

"Let's climb up!" Wanda suggested.

Arnold looked at the tree. "It's too high. We'd
have to fly to get up there."

"That's a great idea!" said Wanda. "We can make something fly and use it to rescue Liz."

Arnold frowned. "I don't think my airplane will ever get off the ground."

"Then let's try something simpler," Wanda said.

What other things fly besides airplanes?

Arnold grabbed a piece of paper. "A paper glider is pretty simple," he said.

"That's true," Wanda said. "And a paper glider can fly. When the air moves across the glider's wide wings, it pushes it up."

Arnold folded the paper into a glider. "This doesn't look big enough to hold Liz," he said.

Wanda aimed the glider at Liz. "It's worth a try!" she said.

Wanda let go of the glider. "Grab onto the glider and fly down, Liz!" she called.

Just then, a gust of wind whipped through the yard.
The glider blew right past Liz.

"Oh, no!" Arnold said. "We'll never rescue Liz now. It's too windy."

Can you think of anything that flies in the wind?

"Arnold, the wind is a great way to make something fly," Wanda said. "Air that moves can push and lift things."

"You mean like when the wind makes a kite fly in the air?" Arnold asked.

"Exactly!" Wanda said.

Arnold looked through his stuff. "I think there's a kite in here somewhere."

Wanda ran down the driveway. The wind picked up the kite and sent it high into the air.

"Grab onto the kite, Liz!" Wanda yelled as she ran.

Arnold was worried. "I think the wind is dying down!"

What will happen to the kite if the wind stops?

19

The wind stopped. The kite stopped flying, too.
"I give up," Arnold said. "We tried a glider. We tried a kite. And we don't have any more helium balloons. How will we fly up and get Liz?"

Suddenly, an acorn fell on Arnold's head.
"Ouch!" Arnold said.

Wanda looked up. "I think Liz is trying to tell us something," she said. "I think she knows a way to get down."

21

Liz pulled a parachute out of her knapsack.

"What's Liz doing now?" Arnold asked.

"I think Liz is going to use air to float to the ground," Wanda said. "The air will push up against the parachute and slow it down as it falls to the ground."

Arnold closed his eyes. "I can't look!" he said.

Liz used the parachute to float safely to the ground.

"Welcome back, Liz," Arnold said. "Now you can be my pilot."

"You don't have to finish your plane," Wanda said. "We made other things fly today."

Arnold looked at Liz. "I guess you're right. Besides, Liz looks like she's had enough flying for one day!"